TAXI

TALES

from the

CAB

RAY FLYNN

AuthorHouse™
1663 Liberty Drive
Bloomington, IN 47403
www.authorhouse.com
Phone: 1 (833) 262-8899

This book is printed on acid-free paper.

ISBN: 978-1-7283-7031-6 (sc)
ISBN: 978-1-7283-7030-9 (e)

Library of Congress Control Number: 2020915670

Print information available on the last page.

Published by AuthorHouse 12/30/2020

author HOUSE®

HWY 49,
AT MOONSHINE ROAD

CUSTOMER QUOTES

"I found out I have a driver's license when I got pulled over."

"It was hilarious. I was all emotional, crying and fighting with my husband. I'm not used to taking strong pain meds."

"I like the old Beverly Hillbillies. Granny and I are best friends."

"I'm going to do as much as I can to cause problems. I really want to fuck with them."

"Thank you for the lovely ride. You're very easy on the eyes."
Then the cross-eyed customer kissed my hand.

"I'm retarded. I mean retired."
I have actually heard two different customers say this over the last five years of driving cab.

"Just because she's crippled, doesn't mean she's old."

"I was a good girl, as far as sex and stuff went, but I'd take all the drugs I could get!"

"There is a line between having self-esteem and being crazy. This woman was in Wal-Mart wearing a fishnet body suit with stars on her nipples. Weighing 300 POUNDS!"

ANANDA VILLAGE
NEVADA CITY, CA

BAT-MITTON

He had been sitting with his girlfriend, when she turned to him and said, "I think there's something in the wood stove." "What?" She says again, "I think there is something in the wood stove." He gets up, opens the door to the wood stove and two bats fly out. His girlfriend is up in a flash, screaming bloody murder. Classic Tom and Jerry scene. Woman on a chair, shrieking. He grabs a tennis racket and starts swinging at the bats as they fly by. As he hits them out of the air, they squeal. His girlfriend is still shrieking. He said this wasn't the only time he hit bats with a racket in his house. One of the side-effects to living in the woods.

BROAD STREET NEVADA CITY, CA

IN THE WEEDS

I realize that marijuana was legalized in our state a few years ago, but it is still strange to see the change. Driving around, I am still laughing at billboards advertising dispensaries and delivery services. I was taking a customer home, out in the sticks, and we drove by a road-side vendor. I usually see a man in a van selling blankets in this area, but today there was also a new guy. He was further down the road, selling plants. My customer said, "he's selling weed starts!" I was surprised and said, " man, people are really getting bold." My customer replied, "well, it IS legal now. At least on a state-level."

JONESIN'

"I've been in jail, smokin' weed rolled in Bible paper."

KIDDIE BOX

One fella said that years ago, he had a roommate who had three children. All young girls. He came home one day to find his roommate's youngest daughter squatting over the cat box, peeing. The older siblings had put her up to it, so all three kids got in trouble. He said that after coming home to that, he had to go out and get a drink.

PERSPECTIVE

"I was raised a Jehovah's Witness. They don't celebrate holidays or birthdays at all. I think it's an excuse to be cheap, really."

ANANDA VILLAGE, NEVADA CITY

TESLA TALE

A customer said that when he was living in Sacramento, many years ago, he got a surprise visit. He had been playing guitar and smoking weed with his door and windows open. When he heard the knock and opened the door, he was surprised to see two members of the band Tesla. They said they could smell his pot smoke down the street and it smelled great. So he shared and they ended up jamming together.

ON LOVE

"I think people say 'I love you' too often. Too freely. Same with 'I'm sorry'."

PISSED

One mustachioed woman told me that she had been homeless for 11 years. On cold winter nights, she would piss herself, just to keep warm. "The problem is, once it gets cold, then you're cold AND wet. So you gotta keep pissing yourself the keep warm."

Side entrance to the Bidwell Mansion in Chico, CA

CUSTOMER QUOTES

"You ever pick up any weirdos in your cab?"

"Wheelchair or no, if I can stand, Imma whoop her ass!"

"When I get home, I'm going to tell her, 'look Mom, I'm tired of your . . . your **shitness**'."

"Indian food looks like regurgitated baby shit."

"I told him, 'don't be a vagina'!"

"I watch Star Trek and think, 'he's Mexican. Spock is a Mexican'."

"I'm going to go to the homeless shelter and sell weed to the homeless. Hang out for awhile."

"Oh my God! Here's the real kicker . . . Hold onto your underwear! They called the cops!"

"My son just got out of jail, because he's a dumbass . . ."

Me - "Isn't 12 old enough to babysit?"
Customer - "Hell yeah! Usually. My niece is dumb as a box of rocks though."

"I feel all loopy. I haven't even taken any drugs yet."

"My caregiver says my room smells bad. I don't know where the smell is coming from. When my cat died, he died under the bed. After I found him, I found a bunch of piss and shit under there too."

SANTA FLAWS

A woman told me that she stopped believing in Santa Claus when she was nine years old. She and her family had moved from a house into an apartment that didn't have a fireplace. She had asked her mom how Santa was going to be able to bring them presents. Her mom replied that, because Santa is magic, he can make himself small enough to fit through the heater vents. She wasn't buying in it and stopped believing in Santa Claus at that point.

MOKSHA MANDIR
NEVAVADA CITY, CA

STICK-HER

I picked up this woman and her three-year-old son. He starts getting antsy in the back, so she hands him a sheet of stickers. He starts peeling off his Ninja Turtle stickers and places them on his shirt. Then he tells her he wants to give her one. So she reaches her hand back and he places a sticker on it. She looks at her hand in amazement and says, "you're so smart son! I saw all those circles on there, but thought it was all one big sticker. You figured out that you can peel the circles off the sheet! You're smarter than me!"

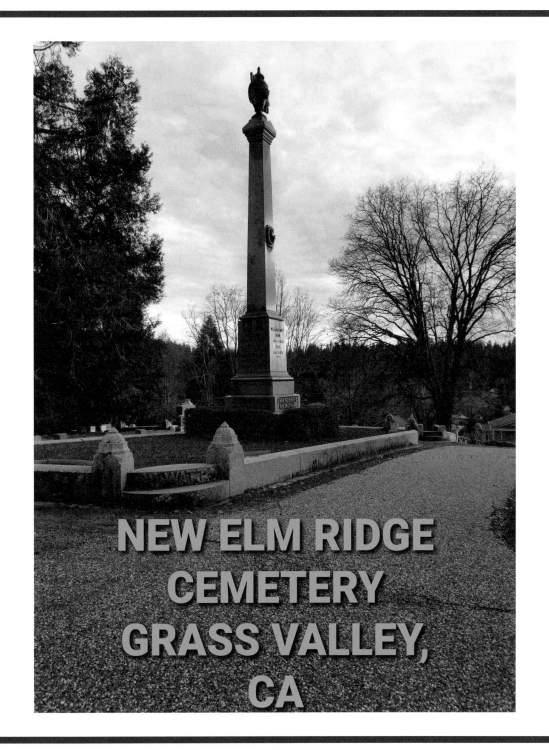

NEW ELM RIDGE
CEMETERY
GRASS VALLEY,
CA

STORY AND SNOOZE

I had a customer on a lengthy ride; he was telling me stories about being a kid and a teenager in Oakland, during the eighties. He said that he used to have a friend who was a DJ, who would play late at night on a local rock station. He and his friends had found a mausoleum in a Jewish cemetery that had an outlet in it. So they would plug in their radio and hang out in the mausoleum at night, drinking beer. During the story, he had nodded off to sleep. I let him be. After a few minutes, he snapped back awake and said, "now what was I lying about?"

OREGON CREEK

WAITING . . .

I knocked on the door and heard, "Just a minute!" I said, "no problem! Cab here." I snapped a picture of a sign in the window and waited. Then I hear through the door, "YOUR CAB'S HERE!" Then a male voice replies, "I'M TAKING A FUCKING DUMP!" The female voice yells his name. He yells back, "HANG ON! I'VE GOT SHIT RUNNING DOWN MY LEG!" I went back to the cab to wait. I had heard enough.

I had another ride at the same address. This time, there was a woman stretched out on the lawn, in a lounge chair, smoking a joint. Perfect.

SOUTH YUBA
RIVER BRIDGE,
HWY 49

TROUBLE

One lady said that she had been up in the mountains, riding snowmobiles with family. She had been on the back of her father-in-law's snowmobile, with him driving. He was a good sized man, who was wearing a big puffy, Michelin Man style jacket. The easiest thing she could grip onto, for safety, was something in his breast pocket. She grabbed on the best she could and they started to go. After a minute he stops and tells her, "Honey, if we get in an accident or something and you end up pulling that flask out of my pocket, we're going to be in real trouble."

SIERRA FOOTHILLS, CA

CUSTOMER QUOTES

"Let me tell you somethin', I'm not sayin' nothin'."

"I told the guy, 'I'll tell you what, don't screw up and I won't kill ya'."

"I remember when coke came out. That was a fun time."

"I don't know all these medical, technical terms, like 'gullet' or 'maw'."

"I'm not supposed to eat before this procedure. I only had a piece of bread, folded in half, with jelly."

"This morning, I went into my room and . . . Well, that's the end of that story."

"I don't know if black people get sunburned, but that Hawaiian girl sure did!"

"The day is early; we have plenty of time to fuck up!"

"My brother's car is held together with tape. I told him he had to take some of that shit off, so I could work on it. You can't open the fuckin' hood."

"You should meet my friend. He has a beard and a mustache. He's a really good guy."

OREGON CREEK,
YUBA COUNTY

DOGGIE DOWN

Another customer said that she had been riding her bike down the street, headed home, when three of her neighbor's dogs came running out to chase her. She stopped and told them to go home. They did, except for one. It stayed in the road and barked at her some more. Then a van came whipping around the corner and speeding down the street. It hit the dog, killing it. My customer had witnessed the gruesome scene, screaming at the driver, but the van kept going. The dog's blood and guts were strewn down the road. That event had happened more than a year prior but had left her traumatized. She had been going to therapy since.

Shortly after that, there was another incident when she had been riding her bike and the same van had come barreling down the street and almost struck her on the side of the road. No stopping or even slowing down. No acknowledgment.

CALIFORNIA

HOOTERS

I helped one of our regular customers into her house, with her things. Once I got her wheelchair over the threshold, I could smell inside. I said cheerily, "your house smells like pot smoke." She exclaimed, "my daughter's so good to me! She rolls my hooters for me in the mornings!" I was cracking up laughing. I hadn't heard anyone use the term Hooter in a long time.

HWY 49, CA

QUITTIN' TIME

A female customer told me how she quit smoking. She had quit buying cigarettes, but her neighbors smoked. She would rob their ashtray at night and smoke their butts. Finally, she had enough of that. So, she grabbed a mason jar and filled it with the contents of the neighbor's ashtray. She then filled it up, the rest of the way, with water. Whenever craving a smoke, she would just crack open the lid on the mason jar and take a whiff of soggy butts and ashes, and that would satiate her craving.

AUBURN, CA
PLACER COUNTY

SUPER BLONDE

One woman's daughter had been in the navy for years. Her job was to load bombs onto jets. She commented on her daughter being super blonde and added that she didn't know why the navy would trust her with the task.

CRYSTAL GOD

One guy had a "seven-year journey with God". On his journey he had been on crystal meth and smoking pot. On seven different occasions he had actually seen God. The first time it happened, he was in a mostly empty movie theater, trying to sit still, when he saw a red light go across the entire movie screen. Then the screen started to piece apart, and he realized what he was looking at. These different pieces on the movie screen, that's where he saw God. It made him a true believer.

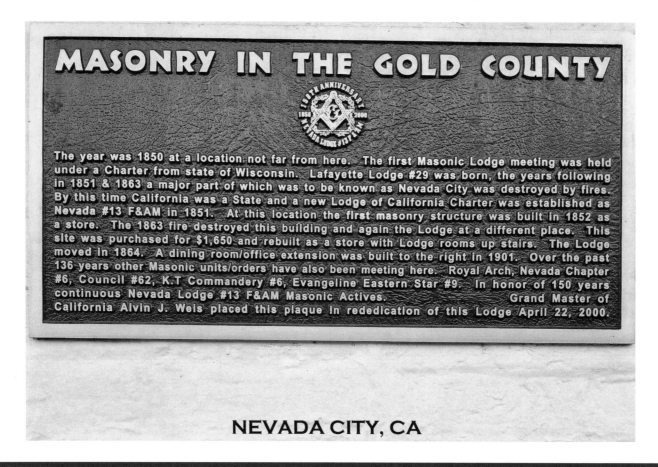

MASONRY IN THE GOLD COUNTY

The year was 1850 at a location not far from here. The first Masonic Lodge meeting was held under a Charter from state of Wisconsin. Lafayette Lodge #29 was born, the years following in 1851 & 1863 a major part of which was to be known as Nevada City was destroyed by fires. By this time California was a State and a new Lodge of California Charter was established as Nevada #13 F&AM in 1851. At this location the first masonry structure was built in 1852 as a store. The 1863 fire destroyed this building and again the Lodge at a different place. This site was purchased for $1,650 and rebuilt as a store with Lodge rooms up stairs. The Lodge moved in 1864. A dining room/office extension was built to the right in 1901. Over the past 136 years other Masonic units/orders have also been meeting here. Royal Arch, Nevada Chapter #6, Council #62, K.T Commandery #6, Evangeline Eastern Star #9. In honor of 150 years continuous Nevada Lodge #13 F&AM Masonic Actives. Grand Master of California Alvin J. Weis placed this plaque in rededication of this Lodge April 22, 2000.

NEVADA CITY, CA

ON MARIJUANA . . .

"I've only tried it two times. Both times I just ate everything in the house, and I do mean EVERYTHING. I was opening all kinds of cans in the pantry, eating butter and mayonnaise by the spoonful. Everything. I never got a high though. My kids said I got ahold of some bunk weed."

CAMPTONVILLE, CA

SAME DIFFERENCE

One of our regulars was talking about how he had been affected by a recent stroke. "I'm the same. Everything about me is the same . . . Except me."

ASS WIPE

"I wipe my ass, so I don't smell like shit. I get tissues wet in the sink, to clean the shit up. Then I use a light cologne. I don't smell like shit, do I?"

CAPTAIN MORGAN

I picked a customer up from a physical therapy facility. When he got settled in, I asked how his appointment went. He exclaimed, "the therapist Captain Morganed me!" I asked what that meant and he said, "I was laying down on the table after a massage. I turned over, onto my back, and he put his leg up on the table, in a Captain Morgan pose! He was wearing shorts and I was laying down, so I could see EVERYTHING. I'm traumatized. He totally Captain Morganed me."

OREGON CREEK
DAY USE AREA

TAHOE
National Forest

YUBA COUNTY, CA

OCCUPYING TIME

I was talking to a customer about smoking. This small, white haired, old man with a cockney accent. He said he only smokes one or two cigarettes a day. I said, "me too. One might think that it would be easier to quit, only smoking one or two. I find that I'm fine during the day when I'm busy, but after work and a meal, I crave a smoke. I think I need to find another way to occupy my time." He said, "well, you could always take-up cocaine."

THIS WILL BE GREAT!

"I tried meth and I was like, 'this will be great! I'll have energy and lose weight! I'll make new friends and have new things to do.' So I did meth for three years and I was like, 'this is fun!' And my family was like, 'we're going to take your kids away.' So then I said, 'I'm done'."

Brownsville, CA

WAIT

I was telling a customer how I had lost a chunk of tooth while eating a sandwich a couple of days prior, and in need of making a dental appointment. She said, "wait. Wait until you find a man with a good job. Cal Trans is a good job. I can show you where to go, to meet a man with a good job like that. Get him wrapped around your finger. Then get him to pay for it."

CUSTOMER QUOTES

"My husband goes to bed before the chickens."

"When I get my disability check, me and you are going to Reno, to the Harley Davidson store!"

"I don't have STDs, but I have everything else wrong with me."

"Used to be, when I saw red and blue lights behind me, I'd hit the gas to get the fuck away. High speed chase and all that."

"Even though I had broken my leg in four places, shattered my knee and my ankle, they took my leg brace when I went into prison. They took it since it had metal in it. I could make a shank out of it and stab someone."

"This girl had big breastie titties and she had a bottle of tequila in there!"

"I'd invite you in for a drink, but I know you won't come inside. So, I'll just have a drink for you."

"How come his eye socket is tighter than my ass?"

"I've got a hatchet and duct tape. Let's go."

"You know Mormons . . . These people, with all their kids, are crazy. They're going straight to Hell. Do not pass GO, do not collect $200. Go directly to JAIL."

NEVADA CITY, CA

SO IN LOVE

I picked up a young woman. She was making out with a guy when I pulled up. As she gets in the cab she says, "he is SO sweet. He is SO in love with me. I love it. I love him. He's so great." We chat for a few. Making pleasant, small talk. Then she gets on the phone and I hear from her end, "hi honey! I'm in the cab. I'll be home soon. Are **you** home?" She's on the phone for about five minutes. When she hangs up, she starts gushing about how great her husband is and how sweet he is for watching their baby while she's out.

FOLSOM, CA

Customer - "I've had seven DUIs."

Me - "How does that happen?"

Customer - "Well, it's really quite easy! I got drunk, then drove. I was trying to help people by giving them rides."

Me - "I mean, I would think that after three, you wouldn't be able to get your license."

Customer - (Laughs) "Oh, I didn't have a license!"

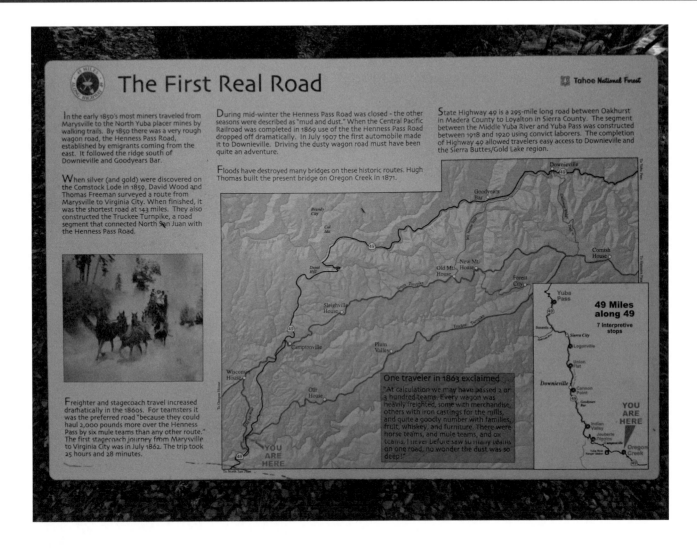

The First Real Road

Tahoe National Forest

In the early 1850's most miners traveled from Marysville to the North Yuba placer mines by walking trails. By 1850 there was a very rough wagon road, the Henness Pass Road, established by emigrants coming from the east. It followed the ridge south of Downieville and Goodyears Bar.

When silver (and gold) were discovered on the Comstock Lode in 1859, David Wood and Thomas Freeman surveyed a route from Marysville to Virginia City. When finished, it was the shortest road at 143 miles. They also constructed the Truckee Turnpike, a road segment that connected North San Juan with the Henness Pass Road.

During mid-winter the Henness Pass Road was closed - the other seasons were described as "mud and dust." When the Central Pacific Railroad was completed in 1869 use of the the Henness Pass Road dropped off dramatically. In July 1907 the first automobile made it to Downieville. Driving the dusty wagon road must have been quite an adventure.

Floods have destroyed many bridges on these historic routes. Hugh Thomas built the present bridge on Oregon Creek in 1871.

State Highway 49 is a 295-mile long road between Oakhurst in Madera County to Loyalton in Sierra County. The segment between the Middle Yuba River and Yuba Pass was constructed between 1918 and 1920 using convict laborers. The completion of Highway 49 allowed travelers easy access to Downieville and the Sierra Buttes/Gold Lake region.

Freighter and stagecoach travel increased dramatically in the 1860s. For teamsters it was the preferred road "because they could haul 2,000 pounds more over the Henness Pass by six mule teams than any other route." The first stagecoach journey from Marysville to Virginia City was in July 1862. The trip took 25 hours and 28 minutes.

49 Miles along 49
7 interpretive stops

YOU ARE HERE

One traveler in 1863 exclaimed
"At calculation we may have passed 2 or 3 hundred teams. Every wagon was heavily freighted, some with merchandise, others with iron castings for the mills, and quite a goodly number with families, fruit, whiskey, and furniture. There were horse teams, and mule teams, and ox teams. I never before saw so many teams on one road, no wonder the dust was so deep!"

CUSTOMER COMPLIMENT

"You have nice teeth. They look strong . . . and pretty white. Your eyes are whiter. Your nails are skin colored."

Be still my heart.

ON MY PORCH

"The last time I got arrested, I was sitting on my porch drinking. The cop pulls up and says, "Mr. _____, have you been drinking?" I told him, 'yeah. That's why I'm sitting on the porch'. I got a drunk in public."

NEVADA CITY, CA

TWEAKER IN A TREE

One of my regulars said that before she moved, her old neighbors had a big pot grow and around harvest time, he would get 'gacked out' on meth so he could stay up all night to watch over his plants. The guy somehow managed to get a loveseat up in the tree, in his yard. So he would be posted up in the tree, with a shotgun, on lookout all night. Watching over his grow in comfort.

NEVADA COUNTY, CA

WITH A 9-YEAR-OLD

My first pick up this morning was a 48-year-old woman in a wheelchair. She said that she had spent 21 years of her life in prison. At one point, she had spent more years of her life in an institution of some sort, rather than out. The first time was when she was 13 years old, it was for stealing and totaling her mother's car. She happened to have a 9 year old in the car with her. She didn't explain why or who the kid was, and I didn't ask. She said that after they crashed her mom's car, they tried to book it, but they couldn't run fast enough. Especially the 9 year old.

HWY 49
NEVADA COUNTY

ROAD RAGE

I had gotten stuck behind a slow mover on a two-lane highway. It didn't take long before my customer started shouting at the truck in front of us, waiving a fist in the air. "What, do ya got a bucket of piss on your passenger seat? Are you afraid to spill it?" I started laughing, because of all the things I've heard people say when road raging, I had never heard that before. She told me that, "that's what my Mom used to say when we were driving. Especially if someone was taking a corner too slow."

OREGON CREEK
COVERED
BRIDGE, CA

OH CRAP

A woman gets in and we start making small-talk. I asked how her holiday was, since Independence Day had just passed. She told me about barbequing with family, kids playing and swimming in a kiddie pool and watching fireworks. After the big display from town was over, she and her grown kids had set off their own fireworks and started taking shots. Shots of tequila, rum, vodka and whiskey. She didn't remember her kids and grandkids leaving. Thankfully, they lived right next door and weren't driving anywhere. Apparently, she had gotten so trashed, that she crapped herself. She went into far too much detail, describing the mess. She had fallen on the floor, and that's where she was when she started coming out of her black-out. In it. She was too wasted to get up and kept slipping in the mess. Eventually she just crawled across her apartment, to get into the shower.

OREGON CITY COVERED BRIDGE, CA

CUSTOMER QUOTES

"I was out jaywalking. Man, there's a lot of traffic."

Me – "Man, what a storm. I've seen a ton of limbs down this morning."
Customer – "Like, legs and arms and everything?"
Me – "Uh, no. Tree limbs. The storm isn't that wild yet."

Customer – "You know what I've always fantasized about?"
Me – "Uuuuuhh . . ."
Customer – "Finding a gypsie's grave and digging it up."

"My son said he felt abandoned, because I left him as a child. He was eight years old. I would leave for a week or two at a time, with my boyfriend. I didn't see anything wrong with it. Still don't."

"You know how I take care of bats? With a tennis racket."

"Larry picked me up today. He said there's cows in someone's front yard, in Olivehurst."
I don't know who Larry is.

"I gave myself a heart attack, so I could get out of jail. It worked."

"My car got repo-ed while my husband was just ten feet away, inside the house. He was too busy smokin' crack on the couch with his buddy, to notice."

DEAD FISH

I picked up a young man about twenty minutes outside of town. We get halfway to town when he yells out, "Ah! I forgot my dead fish! I was going to bring it with me!" Apparently, he had bought a fish from Pet Co two days prior, but it died. He was going to return the fish. I had never heard of such a thing. I never would have thought of returning a dead fish to the pet store. He then proceeded to tell me why he prefers the company I drive for, over the other guys. After getting picked up from the bar one night, he thought the male driver was checking out his girlfriend, who was wearing a short skirt.

"I'm a Christian. I know I shouldn't have punched the guy, but I didn't get arrested. After that, they (the other taxi company), ended up putting cameras in all the cabs."

GRASS VALLEY, CA

CUSTOMER QUOTES

"I can be as patient as pie."

"I like to drink water. Especially after being in the hospital for three days, for heat stroke. I swear by it. It even helps to keep my teeth clean. I haven't had a cavity in 15 years!"

"I've been shot. Twice. Stabbed. Stabbed in the hand. Beaten bloody. Pistol whipped and horse whipped, and now this. They told me I have cancer."

"See that car, the Toyota? It can't catch Covid-19. It can only get the Corolla virus."

"My counselor said he hates tweakers. He prefers heroin heads, because they're more mellow."

"I saw a house for rent, a two bedroom house, for only $400 a month. Either it's an old lady who doesn't know what she has or she's a killer."

"My boss called to ask me why the tape was taped. I cut the receipt tape and taped it back together. I told him, 'you should just fire me'."

NEVADA CITY, CA

OUT TO LUNCH

"I asked a bum out once. This girl was bumming around, in front of the casino. So I asked her if she'd like to go to lunch with me. Have lunch and a beer. And she said no. I guess she could tell I'm not a catch or somethin'." I said, "maybe she just wasn't hungry." "I guess. I guess there's bums out there, that ain't hungry. I just said, 'you know, it's not like I'm just gonna to bend you over the table right there, or something. I just want to take you out to lunch. You don't even have to have the beer'."

I THOUGHT HE WAS GOING TO TELL ME A JOKE

"In every city that has a Martin Luther King Jr Boulevard, those streets always have the highest crime rates. Do you know why?" "Ummm . . . No." "Because that's where all the black people live."

Nevada City, CA

NO RIDE

I picked up a couple that I had dropped off earlier in the day. As they climb into the back, the wife said, "a white Crown Vic pulled into the parking lot, so my husband went up to the window to find out if it was you. He asked the man inside, 'Are you the cab?' And the man told him, 'no. I'm the police.' So thankfully he didn't give us a ride! I told him, 'don't worry about it. We'll wait'!"

OREGON CITY
SCHOOL, CA

ACTIVITY

I picked up a man who was getting around with a walker. His last house was alive with paranormal activity. There were the usual things you hear about. Foot steps down a hall, doorknobs turning and rattling. After a while, things started to escalate. Doors and cabinets opening and slamming closed. The oppressive feeling of being watched. Hearing loudly whispered threats. He told me a story of walking down the hall, to a set of stairs, but before he reached the stairs, an unseen force had picked him up and forcefully slammed him against the floor. Twice. The experience left him with a broken hip and his leg broken in two places. He moved after he had recovered in the hospital. He now lives in a house with several roommates, but to him it's better than going back to that unwelcoming house.

NEVADA CITY, CA

謹向內華遠
縣華僑先驅
者致敬他們
的足跡永遠
的印在斯愛納
的土地上

TO HONOR THE CHINESE PIONEERS OF
NEVADA COUNTY
WHOSE FOOTPRINTS REMAIN FOREVER
EMBEDDED IN THE SIERRA LANDSCAPE

DEDICATED BY:
CITY OF NEVADA CITY
THE NEVADA CITY CHINESE QUARTER SOCIETY
NEVADA COUNTY ARTS COUNCIL
USDA FOREST SERVICE

2005

PAPER PLATE

A customer told me about waring with her neighbor. On one particular day, she was out barbequing and the neighbor had her door open. A screaming match had begun and my customer had gotten so pissed, she threw a stack of paper plates into the other woman's trailer, at her. "So, she called the cops on me. I got arrested and charged with Assault with a Paper Plate. Isn't that ridiculous? Apparently, the judge thought so too. He laughed and threw it out of court!"

CRYSTAL HERMITAGE
GARDENS,
NEVADA CITY, CA

BLACK AND WHITE

A woman and her 17 year old daughter were riding in the back, chatting, when the daughter had said, "y'all are older than me. Can I ask you something? What was the world like before color? Like in the 70's. Did people only have black and white house paint and cars?" Then her Mom asked, "You mean before color TV and color photos?" I was trying to not burst out laughing, so I said nothing. Then the daughter answered slowly, "ohhh. The whole world wasn't black and white then?"

MOHAWK MINE
NEVADA CITY
CA

BREAK IN

I was driving a big woman home from a doctor's appointment. She was telling me about her hip injury and how it happened. Her now-ex-husband had acquired a vial of LSD. After he had been taking doses of it for several days in a row, she had asked him to take a break from it. He was acting crazy. Doing weird things, like digging a giant hole in the yard, so he can make a tunnel under their property. She was in their garage when he blasted her with a fire hose, knocking her to the ground.

Since then, she had moved and was getting medical help for her hip injury. When we start to get close to her place, she asks me to stop at her sister's trailer on the way. She had just realized that she did not have her keys, but her sister had one of her spare keys. I pull up and the trailer is dark. She hands me a flashlight and says to follow her in. I hesitated but followed. She was a customer, after all. I hold a flashlight while she rummages around this dark trailer. After a couple minutes she says she can't find her key. Her sister isn't answering her phone. So we continue on. When we get to her trailer, she tells me that it is padlocked on the inside. She offered me a rickety stepladder and the support of her shoulder. I was really hesitant at this point. She had three little dogs inside. They are all freaking out because Mom's home! She tells me that I'll have to break into the tiny, back window. It is the only one that's not locked. I caved and slowly stepped up on the ladder. She told me to step on her shoulder, to get into the window. I protested because she was injured. She insisted. So, I stepped on her and stretched out to the window. Upon opening it, a painting of Jesus fell and smashed my fingers. I set it aside and started to pull myself in. My hips got stuck. A small, box television fell on my head and suddenly, all the little dogs where licking my face. Super excited and whimpering. I yelled that I was stuck. Then I felt fingers digging into my thighs and a big shove. I was now all the way in and onto the bed. Dogs going nuts. I put the tv back and went for the front door. With her shouting instructions, I got the padlock open on the door. She was grateful. As were the dogs.

I ended up with bruises on my hips, from being stuck in the window, and bruises on my thighs, where she grabbed me. I really hope that was her place.

OREGON CREEK, CA

Printed in the United States
by Baker & Taylor Publisher Services